When Silence Shatters

A Collection of Short Stories

Mahitab Mahmoud

Also By Mahitab Mahmoud

The Color of Our Names

Praise for *The Color of Our Names*

"A culturally grounded and meticulously structured novella… providing a disciplined examination of identity in the face of adversity. The overall impact is strong and memorable."

—IndieReader

"Instead of offering easy resolutions, the story lingers on survival and small acts of defiance… a poignant and ultimately courageous read."

—Readers' Favorite

Paperback ISBN: 978-1970576016
Hardcover ISBN: 978-1970576023
eBook ISBN: 978-1970576009

Dedication

For every voice that was silenced, your silence is heard.

Acknowledgments

To Sherine, my voice when I fall silent. Thank you for being my safe place and for believing in me when I doubt myself. You make me braver. To Yousra, thank you for showing me what friendship rooted in strength and laughter looks like. To my students, you are the heartbeat of my work and the reason I show up with hope. And to my readers, you are not alone. May these stories remind you that your voice matters even when the world attempts to silence it.

Contents

Author's Note

It was the winter of 1996 when I was excitedly waiting for my English teacher to show us a movie on the new VHS located in the two-story colonial-style library in my elementary school building. Unaware that I am a bibliophile, I indulged in sniffing the wood scent of old books and the energizing smell of the new ones while scanning the floor-to-ceiling bookshelves and reading a few blurbs in the hope of finding a new mystery to solve. My heart skipped a beat when Ms. Olga said, "We are going to watch Matilda! Has anyone seen this movie?" "I didn't see it, but I read Roald Dahl's book!" I answered silently. I was a lot more introverted than I am today. All of us were glued to the TV screen. I *silently* yelled: "Matilda! That's me. I, too, have superpowers!"

What an eventful year! The summer of 1996 was the year the Spice Girls released their "Wannabe" song. I remember listening to it, to No Mercy's "Where Do You Go?" and to Mr. President's "Coco Jambo" in my mom's car on our way to the pool. It was also the year that Tupac released his fourth album *All Eyez on Me* (before getting shot later in September); Sabrina the Teenage Witch series debuted on ABC; the Mad Cow Disease was confirmed as transmittable to humans; the O.J. Simpson civil trial for wrongful death began, to name only a few. It was a rollercoaster, way beyond what an 8-year-old could process. Whether it was escapism or denial, I took refuge in books and music. I daydreamed of special powers that could help me save the world. I was the "Matilda" in my family.

I connected with Matilda in so many ways. Her fantasy, magical thinking, and sense of justice matched mine. Reading helped me live in a more decent, parallel world where I can shut a door by staring at it (just like Matilda). It was the same parallel world where I had a sense of moral obligation to right the wrongs around me, including the bullying of other children. Books were my escape from my difficult life into a world where people are kinder to one another. There was an array of feelings that Matilda and other characters expressed on my behalf. They modeled how to liberate myself from social expectations and from other restrictions. They taught me how to set boundaries and honor them, and when to respectfully say "no". Role models are not necessarily family members; a role model can be a teacher, a coach, a neighbor, or a stranger.

The connection Matilda had with Ms. Honey was like mine with Ms. Susan. Ms. Susan supported me and believed in me more than my family did. She understood me and was able to read through me. She also supported me and encouraged me to dream big. I remember when she chose me to rehearse for the narrator role in the

"The Three Little Pigs" play in my kindergarten graduation ceremony. She sewed a red cloak and gave me a long sheet to memorize. I remember telling her that I might forget the words when I am on stage before the audience. She said she would be standing behind the curtains, where no one could see her but me. On the day of graduation, I was surprised at how brave I was while narrating the story. I took a sneak peek at the place where she was supposed to be standing behind the curtains, but I didn't find her. I continued to narrate the story regardless. I could still feel her support even though she wasn't physically there. She wanted me to trust myself when facing the situations I fear the most. I learned to have faith in myself and to appreciate the support that others offer. Ms. Honey did the same with Matilda. She taught her how to face the challenges in her life and how to realize her potential.

Now that I am a teacher, I recall Ms. Olga's question like a voiceover when I ask my own students the exact same one: "Has anyone seen this movie?" I include it in "The Girl Who Can" (Ama Ata Aidoo) lesson to contrast the main characters, Matilda and Adjoa, and see how each one of them advocates for herself. It brings joy to my heart to know that some of my students watched the movie and/or read the book. Sometimes, when a student's face lights up, I can't help but wonder if I might be the "Ms. Honey" in their lives.

I see how role models and books prepared me for the path of resilience. As Tim Elmore once wrote, "Prepare the child for the path, not the path for the child." My teachers, Dahl's characters, and countless other stories prepared me to question silence, resist conformity, and imagine worlds where women and girls could shatter the walls around them.

The women and LGBTQ characters you will meet in this collection live under pressures and expectations that silence them, traditions that confine them, and injustices that bruise them. Yet each one finds a way to resist, to speak, to break the silence. *When Silence Shatters* is not just a title; it is a statement, a promise. These stories may be fictional, but they are born from truths I have lived, witnessed, and carried.

—Mahitab Mahmoud

Stained

It was noon when Mariam and Nadine started their shopping adventure at La Gaité, one of the most populous streets in Ibrahimeya at the heart of Alexandria, Egypt. Until only a few decades ago, it had been a cosmopolitan home for Armenian, Greek, French, British, and other communities who lived with Egyptians in a peaceful, tightly-knit, multinational society with intertwined cultures. Most of them ran their own businesses all around the city. Both young women were deeply influenced by the novels and movies about that time, especially by the anecdotes told by their nostalgic grandparents, parents, and older relatives, whose memories of neighbors, spouses, and business partners of all backgrounds were still vivid and very much alive.

Now it was nearly impossible to walk on the sidewalk of La Gaité because of the dozens of vendors and carts. Pedestrians were forced to walk beside the cars, which moved more slowly than tortoises through the crowds.

"Whenever I come here, I can't help but imagine what it was like in the old days," said Mariam.

"I hope this helps change your mind about traveling," said Nadine.

Mariam gave Nadine a wistful smile before she stopped by a shoe shop, distracted by her own reflection in the glass.

"Nothing would change my mind. The beauty I see is just a reflection of the memories that are stored in my head. The present is distorted, as you can see. I'm not alive here… You know, we loved talking about Alexandria. I mean Alia and me."

Nadine looked Mariam in the eye through the glass, then whispered, "Do you still think about her?"

Mariam sighed. "Well, I've never stopped. It's complicated. I guess love doesn't really die, does it? It stays hidden deep inside, like in hibernation, and comes out when it's triggered," she said in a low voice, after checking both sides to make sure no one was listening.

"Maybe you feel this way because you never really had closure in that relationship."

"That's true. Deep down, I feel she still loves me. That makes it hard to move on. With both of us alive, it's impossible to have closure. Our love is the Catherine-and-Heathcliff kind of love. It's a mixture of passion, fury, infatuation, and obsession."

"Is that why you never get bored of teaching *Wuthering Heights* to your students?" Nadine asked wittily as they resumed walking toward the tram station.

Mariam chuckled softly. "Don't be silly."

"It could be a reason, though. How we feel usually shows up in what we do," said Nadine.

"Maybe… I miss her badly. I see her in my cup of coffee every morning. I go to all the places she loves, hoping I might run into her. I can't get her out of my head. It's as if her soul possessed my whole body and being."

"Do you think she's going through the same thing?"

"She won't allow herself to admit it because she chose the path blessed by her family and society. She quit 'abnormality' after her cousin saw us and threatened to tell her family, so now she thinks she's a hasbian…"

"A hasbian?"

"Shush! Are you crazy? Lower your voice."

"Sorry."

They both looked around to make sure no one had been eavesdropping.

"We'd better not spend the rest of our lives in jail," said Mariam.

Their conversation was cut short by the scream of a teenage girl who felt the heavy hand of a young man gripping her thigh as he passed on his bike. He let her go instantly and tried to ride off, but he couldn't pick up speed in the crowd. His T-shirt was yanked from behind, and he was pulled to the ground by Mariam, who had immediately run him. There were plenty of eyewitnesses who either froze where they stood despite the girl's call for help, or simply pulled out their phones to record what they thought could be an interesting story for social media later that day.

Not far away, a sergeant was handing shopping bags to his driver. After watching the scene, he walked reluctantly toward the harasser, who was now wedged between a car and his bike.

"Thank God you're here," said Mariam to the sergeant, still catching her breath. "This guy harassed this girl."

"He was stalking me down the street. I walked fast but I didn't think he'd have the guts to touch me with all these people around. There are witnesses," said the girl.

The sergeant's eyes swept over Mariam and Nadine from head to toe, like a director appraising a model for his next ad campaign.

"Did he touch you, too?" he asked.

"No."

"Then mind your business. Let him go," said the sergeant before turning to the harasser. "Keep your hands to yourself, son. Leave."

Then, he addressed the girl: "Don't expect to be safe in that T-shirt and mini skirt. What were you thinking? You're a woman. Your parents shouldn't have let you go out in clothes like this. Respect yourself to protect yourself, dear," he lectured.

A group of men among the crowd cheered and whistled as if the women at the scene had just lost some competition. The girl blushed, then left sobbing. Mariam tried to stop her, but the girl pulled away.

"Seriously? So, it's her fault now?"

The sergeant ignored Mariam's question. He glanced at the passersby who stopped out of curiosity. Some were teenage boys, grinning and buzzing with excitement as if they were appearing on TV for the first time. Two of them were recording what she was saying to the harasser—and to those defending him.

"You can leave," the sergeant said to the harasser.

"Thank you, Pasha! You're the best," the young man said. "*Tahya Masr* (Long live Egypt)," he added, grinning. But he still couldn't free his bike from Mariam's grip.

"Get your hands off my bike, *ya helwa* (beautiful)," he said, smiling from ear to ear.

Mariam's frown hardened. She kept her grip on the bike and stared at the sergeant.

"Let him go," the sergeant said firmly.

"There's nothing wrong with what she's wearing. It doesn't give him the right to touch her."

"I'm on my last nerve. Let go of his bike, or I'll arrest you for harassing him."

Nadine leaned toward Mariam's ear. "Let's go, Mariam. The girl already left. It's useless arguing with them."

Mariam shot her a look. "You too? They always win because they're good at intimidating us, but I'm not intimidated, Nadine. This has to stop."

One of the women in the crowd finally spoke.

"Look, dear, sending this young man to prison will ruin his future. He's just a young man like many others who can't afford to get married. All we can do is pray for him and let him go," she said, patting Mariam on the back.

Around her, the spectators nodded in agreement. Mariam just stared, unable to process the words.

"What if it were your own daughter who got harassed?" Mariam asked, fighting to keep her anger under control.

"My daughter would never wear what that girl is wearing."

"See?" said the sergeant. "Now, everybody, move along. The party's over."

"No," yelled Mariam. "This guy is not going anywhere except to the police station."

The sergeant looked at Mariam with beady eyes. "I don't have a police car to take him to the station. All cars are reserved for combating terrorism, not for trivial matters like this."

"This is not a trivial matter," Mariam shot back.

"It is," the sergeant snapped. "We don't have time for this unless it's a rape case—which people don't often report because of the shame." He turned to the harasser. "Get the hell out of here before I change my mind and arrest all of you and say I confiscated drugs."

"I don't take drugs, Pasha. I swear!" the young man said.

"Then leave," the sergeant yelled.

"I'm leaving. God bless you."

The young man sped off on his bike and vanished into the crowd. The others quickly dispersed, frightened by the sergeant's threat. Everyone knew what it meant to anger someone in uniform. Mariam and Nadine stayed frozen, unable to believe he had just gotten away with it.

Mariam glared at the sergeant. "Letting a harasser go unpunished is as horrific as terrorism."

The sergeant glared back. "I'll explain so you learn your lesson," he said. "I saved that girl from the shame of going to a police station. She would've been scolded for pressing charges against a poor man who couldn't resist the inappropriate clothes she was wearing. Understood? Now get out of my way."

The sergeant walked off before Mariam could answer. She just stood there, frozen, staring at his back as he left. Nadine held Mariam's hand.

"You're flogging a dead horse," Nadine whispered. "Let's go. We've got errands to run."

Mariam stood silent, her eyes still fixed on the sergeant until he got into the car and drove away. Nadine squeezed her hand to pull her back.

"Are you okay?" Nadine asked quietly.

Mariam looked at Nadine with an empty expression and started walking in silence. It was one of those times she felt too drained to talk.

***

As soon as Mariam walked into the doctor's office, she went straight to the seat by the small window. It's the first thing she looks for anywhere she goes. It helped her release some of her stress, even though the place itself irritated her. The stale smell of old wooden furniture mixed with ashtray smoke. The TV hanging in the corner of the waiting area, and the decade-old magazines scattered across the table, made her feel stranded in the past. It was a nostalgic yet gloomy setting.

The nurse at the small reception desk was a pregnant woman in her mid-thirties who was always on the phone.

"You can't handle the kids for two hours? What do you want me to do? I'm at work—I'm tired and fed up. There are still patients here. I can't leave now. Are you even listening? I said I'm at work. No… She keeps them all week while I'm here, so giving her a break once a week is the least we can do. … Fine. Drop them off at my mother's."

There were five more people in the room: a couple; a mother and her adult son; and one person everyone—including the nurse, except Mariam—kept staring at. The person in the pink T-shirt and ripped jeans sat with their head down, palms over their knees. Mariam could feel how uncomfortable they were under the couple's whispers and laughter. The mother kept throwing looks of disgust at them, then turned back to scolding her son, who still wouldn't give up heroin. Only Mariam smiled at the person when they finally lifted their eyes. She wished she could tell them they were in the same boat.

The doctor's office door was open, and a man in a suit walked out. Mariam had seen him the previous month. He was a pharmaceutical company representative—the kind who made deals with doctors to prescribe their newly released, often barely tested medications to patients. His company, like many others, offered paid trips, conference sponsorships, office renovations, and expensive gifts to doctors who agreed to sell their products at the expense of patients' health. Apparently, this psychiatrist was giving him a hard time by refusing the offers.

"Mariam," said the nurse. "It's your turn."

Mariam walked into the office. The doctor greeted her with a wide smile. It had been a year since she last saw him. After sitting down and warming up the conversation, she told him what had happened at La Gaité.

"I feel like I was the one who got harassed," Mariam said.

"It's normal to feel this way. You're a feminist—you take it upon yourself to speak up for vulnerable women and defend them when needed," said the doctor.

"It's not about being a feminist. Everybody should do something about this kind of barbarism."

The doctor laughed. "Just choose your battles. You might end up in jail one day."

"Well, what happened today is not the reason I came," she said. "I'm here to ask you a question."

He looked concerned. "What is it?"

"You knew about me from the very beginning, didn't you?"

The doctor opened a drawer and took out a pack of cigarettes.

"Do you mind?" he asked, a cigarette between his lips and his thumb on the lighter.

Mariam hated smoke, but she felt embarrassed to say no.

"I just didn't want you to suffer," he said. "Admitting something like that is dangerous in our society. Since you're bisexual, you have the option to choose the straight path. It's controllable with medication."

"Is it? Do you really think it's a choice?"

"It's the safest thing to do—for your family's sake and for your own safety. You'll be disowned, if you're lucky. Or killed."

"What about my right to be myself? You decided for me when I was still in denial. Is that even professional? Do they teach you to obey homophobic norms at the expense of a patient's trust and freedom?"

"Mariam, I understand you're mad, but please—"

"Excuse me, doctor. It's my say. I'm here to tell you the hormonal medication you prescribed me—which you said was just for depression—did nothing to 'fix' me. It didn't change anything, not one iota. It only numbed me and buried me farther from myself. It made me rot with rage from the inside out. I only started to feel relief when I stopped letting everyone else define me and I let myself exist. I'm not exactly a constant ray of sunshine now, but I'm finally at peace with myself. You stalled my self-acceptance—my only ticket to healing. I hope your conscience guides you in the future."

Mariam stood up. Her words and sudden movement hit him like a bullet in the spine. He panicked for a second, then pushed himself up from his chair.

"Goodbye," she said.

"Take care," he replied.

***

When Mariam got home that night, she took off her clothes and stepped into the bathtub. She faced the showerhead and let the water hit her face as if it were slapping her. It was hard to breathe, but it helped her release some of the tension. Suddenly, someone banged on the bathroom door.

"Mariam, come out! Hurry up!"

"What's wrong?"

"You're on TV!"

Mariam didn't understand. She thought she'd misheard what Manal said. She dried off quickly and stepped out. The TV was blasting. It was her mother's favorite show, *The Truth*.

"*Ya* Mariam!"

Mariam rushed to the living room, where Manal was. Manal turned the volume up even though it was already too loud.

"You're on TV!" Manal yelled furiously. "Do you care to tell me what happened? How is your mother the last one to know?"

Mariam froze when she saw a video of herself arguing with the sergeant on screen. She didn't answer.

"The video, which went viral on social media this evening with nearly one million views in just a few hours, was recorded by an anonymous eyewitness. We'll play it again until we manage to reach any of the parties involved to comment. We've already called the sergeant several times, but he's not answering," said the host. "We'd like to know your opinion, dear viewers. Please call us at the numbers shown on the screen. Actually, someone is joining us now to tell us what she thinks. Madam Hanadi? You're on air now. What do you think of the whole situation?"

"Mr. Waked, there is no need to hear from those disgraceful women who stood up to the sergeant," Hanadi began. "They clearly missed a proper upbringing, and now they've stained their reputations forever. How dare they question the sergeant like that? I am sure none of their parents raised them properly."

Manal shot Mariam a long, reproachful look, then turned back to the TV.

"They're absolutely ill-mannered and a shame to our society. Our customs and traditions don't allow women to raise their voices like that, to wear such demeaning clothes, or to argue with our police. God bless the police and the army," Hanadi added.

Manal muted the TV and turned to Mariam.

"Don't you always say that people should mind their own business? Then why aren't you doing the same? Don't you see how contradictory this is? It only gets you in trouble. What am I supposed to tell people when they ask me what you did?"

"Mama, this is my business. Women in our society are taught to blindly obey, to zip their mouths, and not to defend themselves because men are always right. Everybody needs to stop this abuse. I don't care what people say."

Mariam grabbed her phone from the couch and unmuted the TV.

"We have another phone call," said the host. "It's Dr. Salwa, the head of the *Imsek Mohtaharresh* (Catch the Harasser) campaign. We're glad you joined us to comment on the incident."

"Hello, Mr. Waked. First, I would like to thank the courageous young woman who stood up to both the harasser and the sergeant," said Dr. Salwa. "With all due respect, his reaction was totally unacceptable and destructive. She did what every woman should do when her rights are violated. I hope you can help us reach her. Second, we have contacted the Attorney General's office and requested an inquiry into the sergeant's blatant intimidation of that woman and his unjustifiable defense of the harasser. How could he let him go? How could he blame the girl who was harassed and talk her out of reporting him? Does he understand how traumatic this is for her?"

At this point, Mariam looked at Manal with raised eyebrows and the beginning of a smile. Manal rolled her eyes and turned back toward the TV.

"Pardon me, Dr. Salwa," said the host, "but don't you think he had a point about her clothes being inappropriate?"

"There is no excuse whatsoever for men to verbally or physically harass a woman," said Dr. Salwa. "Blaming the girl, and giving men excuses like poverty or not being able to afford marriage, is an unhealthy tradition our society has been nurturing for ages. It's time we put an end to this."

"She's dreaming," Manal muttered.

"Well, at least she's doing something, Mama."

Mariam felt her phone vibrate. She unlocked it and saw multiple missed calls and messages from Nadine, friends, relatives, and workmates—but one name sent a cold shiver through her. At the same time, the landline started ringing. Manal picked up.

"Yes, we're watching it now. I told her so! You know how stubborn she is," Manal said, staring at Mariam. She covered the receiver. "It's *Khalto* Samira," she whispered.

Saved by the bell, Mariam—nervous but relieved—slipped out to her room while Manal was busy on the phone with her sister. Mariam hated attention. Being on TV made her feel exposed. What made her even more anxious was seeing Alia's name on her screen.

"What happened? Where are you now?" Alia had texted.

"I'm okay. At home," Mariam replied.

"I got so worried about you when I saw you on TV."

Mariam smiled. She didn't know how to answer that. The chat showed "Alia is typing." Then it disappeared. Then it came back. Then disappeared again.

Finally, Alia sent: "I know I said it's over and that I'm not as brave as you are, but when I saw you today I wished I was with you. Maybe you can teach me how to free myself from this fear."

Mariam smiled. "I wrote you a poem, Alia," she typed. She sent the poem she'd been keeping in her notes.

A Story of You and Me

I'm a mother's pride and a society's shame

I'm a woman no one could tame.

Behind the chains of my name,

a rainbow flag and a burning flame—

For I'm the deviant a society would blame,

I'm a paradox in a hollow frame.

A sinner, they claim.

Hell, no!

For I'm the earth, sun, and sea,

I'm the antonym yet synonym of free.

I fly from tree to tree,

Mahitab Mahmoud

And I dare them to catch me.

If I'm their enemy then let it be—

No labels could ever define me.

I abide by no rules except integrity;

My story is up to me,

written then set free.

It's a story of you and me,

And of sharing love and equity,

fighting the evil side of humanity

in face of their fallacy and sugarcoated hypocrisy.

The foundation of disparity,

a fragile, unbreakable vanity.

Hurt, but still capable of clarity—

let's heal what's been shattered in hostility.

Alia read the poem. She kept typing and deleting what she typed until she finally sent Mariam: "...."

"Ready to start tonight?"

"Yes, I am now."

The Niche

You're not who they think you are, you're not who they wish you were, and you're not who they want you to be. You know this by heart, even while living in a society where stale traditions, norms, and social codes still rule. There are bundles of nonnegotiable labels with price tags that dictate your value, reputation, social image, and future. They're a lot like the "if-conditional rules" you were taught in school—supposedly simple equations that predict your past, present, and future, sometimes from the cradle to the grave.

"Farida!" your mom yells.

You pretend you didn't hear her, because you know why she's calling you.

"Did you take the china set out of the *niche*?" she asks.

You forgot to do what she asked. But anyway. Back to the thoughts you're writing in your journal.

It still bugs you how a large part of society believes that if you're outspoken, then your mom has failed to raise "a good girl." If you're still single by the time you graduate from college, then your chances of getting married are already low. If you turn 30, aunties, neighbors, and friends start pitying you because, according to them, it's too late for you to be chosen by a man—and your only option to free yourself from the label *'anis* (spinster) is to accept offers from any man, even if he's two or three decades older than you.

If you live alone, then you're a promiscuous woman other people are warned to stay away from—especially if they don't want their husbands to be "stolen." If you're a divorcée, it's even worse: an array of accusations is thrown at your face and behind your back. If you decide to raise the flag of "single and proud," you're called a loser who failed to attract suitors. If you're independent and strong-willed, you intimidate the suitor's mother, who immediately decides you have loose morals. Men who are drawn to you usually seek pleasure, not commitment, because they know you're difficult to bend. If you're highly educated, your chances drop even more, because you're capable of arguing with reason—something some men pretend to like and secretly fear. Those same men who act offended by your "attitude" don't take "no" for an answer.

And the list of ifs goes on…

"Faridaaaa!!" This time she's not just calling. She's screaming.

"Not yet!" you answer, rolling your eyes. You never have time for yourself in this household. Also, you've always wondered who on earth was bored enough to come up with the niche idea in the first place—that expensive, engagement-spoiler piece of furniture that displays two to five different sets of cups and plates, along with small, useless statues and toys people gifted you on the *sobou'* (the seventh-day baby celebration). You can't help but imagine the pleasure of smashing a couple of plates on the suitor's head.

"Yalla! They'll ring the doorbell any minute. Go wipe them with the rag I left you on the *sufra*."

The *sufra* is the niche's solid companion: a round, square, or rectangular table with four to eight furnished seats. Both live together in the same restricted area that nobody dares approach for fear of breaking their mother's rules. A big "DO NOT TOUCH" sign would be perfect for that room.

"Also, make sure Nesma's ready. Today's her day, so don't spoil it. I know you," your mother adds.

The truth is, you wish you could spoil it, because you don't buy this whole idea of a woman getting engaged to a man she met for five minutes last week and won't even see again for six more months until the wedding day.

Mo'men and Nesma met at a café, in the presence of both mothers, of course. Now they're coming to make an official proposal, discuss the dowry and all the standardized marriage details, then recite Al-Fatiha once they reach a deal. Everything has to move quickly before Mo'men goes back to Dubai next week.

After all, as they say, "the shadow of a man is better than the shade of a wall."

Naturally, your mother agreed right away. Nesma has just graduated, gone to a series of weddings for friends and cousins, and still didn't "catch" anyone—until Auntie Khayreya, the lifelong matchmaker, called with the good news: a respectable, religious accountant working in Dubai, looking for an Egyptian wife to fulfill his mother's wish. How could your mother possibly turn down a gift she believes was sent by God? She hasn't even told your late father's family yet, in case his sisters get jealous—their daughters are still single.

"Farida, why aren't you wearing makeup? You're going to meet them with this bare face?" your mom asks, horrified like she just watched a car crash.

"Mama, do I look like I care? To hell with what they think. Also, they're here for Nesma, not for me."

"For God's sake, Farida, have mercy on me. I don't have time for your endless arguments. Do as I say. Go put some blusher on your face. Everything has to be perfect."

She doesn't understand that you'd rather look sick than wear makeup. Besides, the way she looked you up and down made your anger rise. You can already smell her plan: to present a second "perfect" daughter, just in case the suitor's mother is shopping for two brides. A buy-one-get-one-free offer. Your mother is desperate to get you married before your sister to shut down gossip. You turn around and head to your room to make it look like you're going to do what she said—and then you don't.

You've always felt that marriage is more transaction than love. The suitor just has to meet minimum requirements: an apartment, a full-time job, and a wedding ring. A car is a bonus, even if it's from the 70s or 80s. It doesn't matter if he's divorced. It doesn't even matter if you're going to be his second, third, or fourth wife. Your family will still bless the marriage—if you're already over 30, or a widow, or a divorcée. Any man is flawless as long as he can afford the initial costs. It all lives inside those unspoken equations, those unquestionable beliefs.

"Farida!" your mom hisses in a harsh whisper. "I can hear their footsteps. Hurry up!"

"Mama, I'm sure they know how to ring the doorbell. Rest assured." You don't like giving too much attention to the stranger who is essentially here to purchase your sister, but you do feel a mix of pity and guilt when you see the nervous excitement in your mom's and Nesma's faces.

The doorbell rings. Your mother hurries to open it while you and your sister stand behind her to "welcome" the guests. The suitor's mother walks in first, followed by Mo'men. The father isn't there because he works in Saudi Arabia and only visits once a year. After all, nothing is wrong with a man except his wallet.

As long as a father or husband wires money home, there's no "need" for the family to join him. Even if the husband is cheating on his wife, it still doesn't matter—as long as it's not announced and it doesn't affect the family's image. Some wives prefer to let sleeping dogs lie.

After shaking hands with the mother, you extend your arm to shake hands with Mo'men. He looks at your hand without offering his.

Nesma jumps in right away to explain, "He doesn't shake hands with women because it's haram."

What provokes you even more is that he doesn't apologize.

Afraid of whatever you might do next—and desperate to cover the awkwardness—your mother raises her voice brightly: "Please, come into the salon!"

You stay where you are while they all walk into the salon. You wonder if God truly prefers the humiliation you just felt, as a woman simply trying to politely shake hands with a man you have zero sexual interest in, over this man's "piety." Which is more sinful: hurting someone's dignity, or shaking hands?

Your mother decides to break the ice by announcing that Nesma is the one who helps her most in the kitchen. She's very good at cooking and doing house chores. This information is offered like a warranty—proof that the suitor made the right choice. It reminds you of what a salesperson does to convince a customer to finally buy, so they can end their window-shopping tour.

"What about Nesma's sister?" asks Mo'men's mother with a sly smile.

"What about me?" you say.

You hate when people ask about you but direct the question to someone else, as if you're not in the room.

"I mean," she says, "do you cook and clean like Nesma?"

You look her directly in the eyes with a contempt so obvious that she raises both eyebrows, then stares at your mother for a few seconds. You and your mother answer at the exact same time:

You: "Of course not."

Your mother: "Yes, of course!"

Your mom forces a laugh and says, "Farida does some housework, but lately she's very busy with her studies and work duties."

Unexpectedly, Mo'men breaks his silence to ask your mother, "Is she still studying? Isn't she 32 years old or something?"

That does it. The question is for you, but he throws it at your mom, and he makes sure to highlight your age.

"What does my age have to do with studying?" you ask, calm and sharp.

"Well, I just couldn't imagine that a woman who graduated from college more than ten years ago would still be interested in studying unless she's either a nerd or just… still single," he says, smirking like he's proud of himself, looking around for agreement.

"Well," you say, eyebrows raised, "'nerd' is the word people like you use for anyone who managed to enjoy something you struggled to pass."

It takes him a second to process that. He looks at his mother, who is clearly realizing she hasn't found her son a wife with a "well-mannered" sister. Your mother and Nesma both clear their throats and laugh like you've made a joke. Unlike you—and unlike your late father—that's their defense mechanism. They evade instead of confront. Your father always taught you to speak your mind.

"You're ruining this girl," your aunts used to tell him. "You're teaching her things she shouldn't know, even when she grows up."

"I'm not ruining her," he'd reply. "I'm making her independent. I won't live forever to protect her. These girls have to protect themselves, and their only means is education."

Mo'men decides to recover his pride by changing the subject—with something even more insulting.

"So," he says, "how many people have you run over so far while driving?"

Everybody laughs. Including your mother. She can tell this man is declaring war, but all she can do is laugh like she's on his side and silently pray you won't kill him.

You stare with an expressionless face, anger boiling in your chest. He reminds you of those men who almost run someone over in traffic, and even when they're 100% at fault, they refuse to apologize—just because they realize the other driver is a woman. Some shake their heads in contempt; others curse the woman and her absent father or husband, who "must have bought her the car."

"You should ask that question to chauvinists like you who don't read," you say evenly. "You probably lay newspapers on the *sufra* under your lunch plates without even opening them."

This time, nobody laughs.

They all stared at you in disbelief until Mo'men finally blurts out, trying to win on volume, not logic: "You must be talking about Western women, because Egyptian women are bad drivers."

You're about to answer, but he talks over you, as if he's on stage in a one-man show.

"You women want everything. You're never satisfied. Isn't it enough that we allow you to work—despite how intolerable you are—and you still insist on showing up in places where you don't belong, places where we're supposed to get a break from you?"

The word "intolerable" makes you think of Mr. Darcy in *Pride and Prejudice*.

"Why do you sound like you're the one who gave women their rights?" you ask. "Women and men are equal, whether you like it or not."

"Men and women are not, and will never be, equal," he says. "Your only role in this life is to cook and raise children. You're not even good at both, but at least you can give birth."

His voice rises with every word, desperate to win before time runs out.

"Well then," you say, "why marry at all if you're that angry at women?"

"I won't," he snaps. "At least not from this disgraceful household."

He stands up. His mother shoots up right after him, like a shadow.

You laugh.

"You're right, son," his mother says. "Let's go. There are no wives for you in this shameful place. I'll find you a respectable family elsewhere."

They pick up the box of chocolates they brought and head for the door without even answering your mother, who's scrambling: "Please wait. There's a misunderstanding. Farida is just like this. Ignore her. Nesma didn't say anything. Wait!"

They hurry down the stairs like the apartment is on fire. Your mother shuts the door and spins around, eyes blazing.

"Are you happy now? He wasn't even coming for you!"

Nesma has already started crying.

"Answer Mama! Are you happy now that you turned my engagement into a contest?"

"Haven't you heard the insults?" you say. "You should be thankful you didn't fall into that trap. He's a devil in disguise."

"There was nothing insulting about what they said or did. YOU are the only devil here. You provoked him and brought out the beast inside."

"Thank God you noticed there's a beast inside."

"We all have beasts inside. You're the one who called his out. How could you do this to us? I'm your sister. Is it because I was getting married before you? Of course you're not getting married—not with that attitude. No man will ever take you. You're miserable, and you want everyone around you to be just as miserable as you are."

Your mother nods. "I agree with your sister. You're selfish and cold-hearted."

You don't answer.

What really hurts you is your sister's blindness. Their accusations don't surprise you. After all, they don't know how much you suffered to earn that "cold-hearted" label. Her words drag you back six years—to an appointment with your psychiatrist. You were sobbing nonstop, begging for help to become bold and outspoken because you were tired of being fooled by people you loved. He promised you progress, with medication and self-empowerment. He told you that one way to know you've learned a lesson in life is that you can finally see the whole situation from every angle. You gain shortcuts and answer keys. You can take a different road next time. You walk away with a sly smile that only comes with a certain maturity. That's when you know you're leveling up.

Now you don't know if your mother's words should please you or scold you. You don't know if you should feel victorious for finally letting your mind lead, or guilty for arriving at a kind of bitter clarity that makes the people around you hate you. You don't know whether to feel ashamed for "ruining" your sister's engagement or relieved for saving her from a bleak future.

They don't know about the volcano inside you that finally erupted. They don't know about the battles you fought alone, trying to fit into an unpleasable society. They don't know how many times you felt like you were living underwater, unable to breathe, until you realized no one was going to pull you out but you.

You're still not sure if knowing too much in this society is a curse or a blessing.

You don't answer their last words. You choose silence.

Silence is multifunctional. It can be an attitude, an answer, a warning, a way to avoid a fight, a sedative, and a secret keeper. Silence is the mute heart, the lonely ache, the hidden feeling, the guilty conscience, the disappointment, the shame, the private victory. Silence is "sorry," "don't leave," "help," "forgive me," "miss you," "love you," and "shut up." Silence can carry messages more eloquent than the best public speaker. It's a language no one but its users can hear.

The problem is they don't understand your silence; they don't speak your language. You're not sure they even see your intention. The only thing you're sure of is that they don't really know who you are.

The Dolls Theater

Malika and her brother, Seif, had been waiting for that day for months. It was finally *Eid al-Fitr*.

In the morning, their mother, Hala, prepared tea with milk in their favorite Looney Tunes mugs, along with a large plate of homemade *kahk*, petit fours, and cookies in all the flavors they loved. They were especially excited to taste the ones they had shaped with their own hands the night before (the last night of Ramadan). It was Malika's first time fasting until 1:00 p.m.—except for the days when she had a bad flu—so that next year she could try to fast all the way until sunset. Seif, who was three years older, had already managed to fast from sunrise to sunset for the second year in a row.

"It's time to get ready," said Hala.

"Will we go to Sindbad after visiting *teita* (grandma) Latifa?" asked Malika.

Hala looked at Tarek, their father. He nodded with a gentle smile.

"Yes, *habibti* (my love)," she said.

"Yaaaaay!" both kids shouted.

"Hurry up. Go put on your new Eid clothes."

It had become their routine to spend a couple of hours at their grandmother's place. *Teita* Latifa was Malika's favorite person in the world. There was a special bond between them—a closeness neither of them ever seemed to get enough of. Malika's attachment to her grandmother made Hala feel two things at once: jealousy and fear. She worried that Latifa's stories about "the old days" and her freer way of living would get into Malika's head and change the kind of woman Malika would become.

Malika loved listening to *teita* Latifa's stories about how wonderful life had been in Egypt up until the late 80s and early 90s, before so many Egyptian men started traveling abroad to make money.

"They worked in Saudi Arabia, Kuwait, Yemen, and other Arab countries," Latifa had told her once. "And they came back with ideas—conservative, religious ideas from back then. They started urging women to wear hijab, long loose skirts, long sleeves. All of a sudden, people were on TV and in mosques talking about what was haram, what women shouldn't wear, how women shouldn't walk, what makes society sinful and brings God's anger."

Then she'd paused, realizing Malika wouldn't understand all of it yet.

"*Teita*, why do women like Mommy wear hijab?" Malika had asked.

"To cover their hair."

"Why do they cover their hair?"

"They say it's sinful to show it to men because it attracts men's attention."

"Then why don't men cover their hair, too?"

Latifa had to hold back a laugh. "Trust me, honey, I asked the very same question to anyone who told me to cover my head. You're such an intelligent girl."

"Do I have to wear it when I grow up like Mommy?"

"No, *habibti*. Don't let anybody force you to do what you don't want. You're a free, strong girl," Latifa said, pulling Malika into a hug. Then she opened her closet. "Do you see these clothes, Malika?"

Malika stared, open-mouthed, at the row of colorful dresses, skirts, pants, and blouses. "Wow."

"I used to wear all of these," Latifa said. "Imagine? Nobody dared to harass me—not with words, not with hands. People were polite and well-mannered. No one bothered anyone. Even when people flirted, they did it in a respectful way. The ugly exceptions were rare. I'd walk with my golden hair on my shoulders, in a sleeveless top and a miniskirt, and not one person said an offensive word, dear."

"This is great. Do you still wear them, *teita*?"

"No, darling," Latifa answered, her voice heavy.

"Why? They're so chic."

"I wish I still could. I can't, for many reasons. First, I'm old now, as you can see. People would stare and laugh at me in the street, because they don't mind their own business. Second, times changed. People changed. They wouldn't accept seeing an old woman dressed like that. They barely accept it from younger women. Your own parents think I'm sinful just because I still refuse to put on a headscarf."

"You're not old, *teita*. You're beautiful," said Malika, rushing to hug her.

"You're the beautiful one, honey. I'm keeping all these clothes for you to wear when you grow up. They're all yours."

"Wow! Thank you so much, *teita*."

"You're welcome, *habibti*."

Malika stared at her grandmother's face for a few seconds like she was trying to memorize it.

"You know? I don't like headscarves either. Mommy looks way better without it, but please don't tell her I said that."

Latifa laughed softly. "Whatever we say to each other stays between us. I'll never spill the beans."

She winked at Malika—then noticed Hala standing in the doorway.

"It's time to go, Malika," Hala said, her face flat.

After they stepped out of the bedroom, Hala leaned toward Tarek and whispered—loudly enough that Malika could hear, because she was right behind them: "If you don't tell your mom to stop talking to Malika about hijab and clothes, I swear she won't see her again. This is my daughter, not hers. May Allah forgive your mom and guide her to the right path."

The smile vanished from Tarek's face like a drawing in sand right before a wave washed over it. While Latifa was walking them to the door and kissing her grandchildren goodbye, she noticed the worry on her son's face.

"*Rabbena yenawwar baseertkom* (May God enlighten your vision)," she said in a calm, steady voice. She waved them off as they went down the stairs.

***

Like every Eid, Tarek took Hala and the kids to Sindbad—the toy store down the block from *teita* Latifa's place—where Malika and Seif could choose toys using their *eidiya* (the money given to kids on Eid by parents, grandparents, uncles, and aunts). Malika and Seif were always amazed by the shelves and shelves of colorful boxes. When they arrived, their parents reminded them that each of them could pick only one toy.

They started out in the girls' section, where everything was pink: dolls, stuffed animals, makeup kits. Seif ran straight to the boys' section to look for the same plastic gun he had wanted last Eid but couldn't afford then, because he had already chosen a remote-control car. Malika wasn't interested in buying a doll this year. She was more curious about whatever was in the boys' section, so she followed Seif.

Tarek stood at the cashier's counter talking to the cashier about prices, while Hala kept an eye on the kids.

"Why didn't you get a doll?" Hala asked.

"I don't want to," Malika said.

"You know, I grew up watching a really interesting TV show called *The Dolls Theater*. I'm sure you would've loved it."

"I don't like dolls. They're dull."

"They're not dull."

"Peow! Peow! Peow! Peow! Peow! Drop your weapon and show me your hands!" shouted Seif, pointing the toy gun at Malika.

"Wow! Can I hold it, please?"

"Okay. Just be careful."

"Is it real?" Malika asked, eyes glowing.

"It is, of course," Seif said, with full confidence.

Hala chuckled. "No, honey. It's just a toy."

Seif grinned like a little cartoon villain. "It's for boys only anyway."

"Why not for girls too?" Malika asked, hurt.

"Girls don't carry guns. They can't, because they'll definitely miss the target and cry like babies, the way you do," Seif said.

"I don't cry like babies!" Malika shot back. "Mommy, please tell him."

She looked straight at Hala, waiting for backup.

"That's enough," Hala said. "Malika, there are lovely dolls in the other section. They come with extra dresses and makeup cases. Go look at them before pappy tells us it's time to go."

"No. I don't want a doll. I want a gun."

"A gun? Of course not."

"Why not?"

"It's for boys, honey. It's also violent for you."

"But Seif is buying one, so how come it's not violent for him?"

Hala hadn't seen that one coming. She stuttered, paused, then raised an eyebrow.

"Asking too many questions is impolite. Remember?"

"I'm asking one question, Mommy. Why is it violent for me but not for him?"

Hala stared at Malika, feeling cornered. "There are no toys for you this Eid," she said, loudly enough to get Tarek's attention from across the store.

"Why?" Malika asked.

"Because you're asking too many questions, as usual. I told you this is called arguing, and it's bad. This is bad behavior."

"I'm not arguing, Mommy. I just want to understand—"

"You know what my father did when I once asked him why he was only taking my brother to the café at night?" Hala cut in. "He locked me in my room until the next day and told the whole house not to talk to me."

"Why didn't he answer your question instead?"

Hala was glaring at her when Tarek walked up. He didn't know the context, but he recognized his wife's angry face, and to him that face always meant Malika must have done "something."

"I second your mom's words. Let's go," he said.

"But pappy, I didn't get a toy—"

"ENOUGH," Tarek snapped.

"That's Latifa's effect," Hala muttered under her breath.

They all moved toward the cashier—except Malika. She didn't follow.

Unanswered questions were one of her biggest pet peeves. Hala turned and realized Malika wasn't with them. Panic flashed across her face. She rushed back down the aisles, calling Malika's name over and over. She finally found her standing in front of a shelf of puzzles, holding one quietly.

"Where have you been? Why didn't you answer when I called your name?"

"I don't know," Malika said. "I'll take this puzzle."

It was one of those moments Hala couldn't read her daughter at all. She couldn't understand how a six-year-old could keep such a straight face when she was hurting—maybe because Hala didn't understand that even a little kid can have her pride broken.

"Okay. We'll take it, even though you don't deserve it," Hala said, flipping the box over to look at the pictures of animals on the back. "Let's go."

On their way to the car, Seif said, "I'll sit next to pappy. It's my turn. You sat there on the way to the store."

"Alright," Hala said.

Malika heard them, but didn't say anything. She already knew Seif always got the front seat next to their father. She had given up on that fight.

In the car, Malika sat in the back with Hala. She avoided looking at her mother the whole ride home. Her small fingers hooked around the edge of the window as she watched the city sliding past in her side view—until she suddenly screamed.

"NO! NO!"

She burst into loud crying.

"What's wrong?" Hala asked, panicking.

"There's a dead kitty…" Malika tried to say, but she couldn't catch her breath through the crying.

"Are you serious? We almost got into a car crash because of your scream!" Tarek yelled.

Hala just stared at Malika.

Seif said, in a flat voice, "Those stupid things keep running across the road. They deserve to die."

Tarek muttered to Seif, "I think I've heard those words before, Mr. Parrot."

Seif giggled at being called out for repeating his father.

After a few breaths, Malika screamed, "They are NOT stupid, and they DON'T deserve to die!"

"Malika, I don't want to hear your voice today. We've had enough," Hala snapped.

"What did I do?"

"ENOUGH."

"Shut up, Malika. We don't want to hear your voice," said Seif.

"Seif," Tarek cut in. "Don't interrupt your mom while she's talking."

He was trying hard to hold himself together. He reached for the control and rolled Malika's back window up from his side of the car door.

"You've been disobedient, Malika," he said. "You're not going out tomorrow. Only Seif and I will."

"Yaaaay! Can we go to McDonald's, pappy?" Seif shouted.

Hala silently poked Seif from behind. She didn't like the idea of eating out, not with everything she heard on TV about fast food. As for Malika, she dissolved into tears and kept sniffling until she cried herself to sleep.

***

The next morning, Tarek dropped Malika and Seif off at the school gate like always. Seif was grumpy, like always. During the morning line-up to salute the flag, he would usually hide his head behind whoever was standing in front of him so the teachers wouldn't catch him talking or laughing.

For Malika, school was her second safe place after *teita* Latifa's apartment. She loved her teachers, especially her English teacher, Ms. Nour.

That morning, Ms. Nour was reading the class a story that mentioned an apple falling from a tree. It reminded Malika of the Adam and Eve story that Mr. Ali, the Islamic religion teacher, had told them. He'd used it to show "how cunning the devil is."

Malika raised her hand.

"Do you have a question, Malika?" asked Ms. Nour.

"Yes, please," Malika said.

"Go ahead, dear."

"Mr. Ali told us that Adam and Eve were married. Is that right?"

"Yes, dear."

"Does that mean they're the parents of all human beings?"

Ms. Nour smiled. "I guess so."

"This means all human beings are brothers and sisters," Malika continued. "So why do people get married when they're actually siblings?"

Ms. Nour's smile grew wider. She walked to Malika's desk and kneeled next to her. "This is a smart question, Malika. You're such an inquisitive girl."

Malika looked at her, confused. "Am I?"

"Of course you are. I'm so glad you ask questions that show how eager you are to learn and understand."

"Is asking questions a good thing or a bad thing?"

"It's a good thing for sure."

"Then why do Mommy and Pappy hate it when I ask questions?"

The smile on Ms. Nour's face started to fade. "Do they?"

Malika frowned and nodded hard. "Mommy says I'm disobedient because I ask many questions. She also says good girls don't argue."

The look on Ms. Nour's face puzzled Malika.

"Did I say something wrong? I'm very sorry. Mommy says I need to filter my mouth."

"No, honey. You didn't say anything wrong," whispered Ms. Nour. "Let's postpone our interesting chat to break time, okay?"

"Okay," Malika said, a little sadly.

***

During break, Nour went to the secretary's desk outside the principal's office and asked to speak with her. The secretary went in first, then opened the door for her.

Mrs. Tafida's office was large and overflowing with crystals, medals, photos of her with teachers and students, trophies, flower vases, a round table, chairs, a couch, and a huge flat-screen TV. Nour couldn't help wondering why a principal needed a TV in her office.

"Hello, Ms. Nour. Please sit and tell me what's urgent," said Mrs. Tafida.

"Yes," Nour began. "Malika—one of my students in Grade 1— is showing clear symptoms of depression. Apparently her parents are putting her under a lot of pressure. They rebuke her for asking questions when she needs to understand something."

"This is what you consider urgent, Ms. Nour?" asked Mrs. Tafida with a smile Nour could tell was fake.

"Yes, Mrs. Tafida. Malika is a prodigy. Her parents seem to be unintentionally crushing her curiosity. This girl could have a limitless future. We can't let them bury her potential."

"We are not her parents, Ms. Nour. We don't even have social services to help the girl. You know how it is in this country. Parents can do whatever they want to their kids and get away with it. Thank God none of them is abusing her."

"This is abuse, Mrs. Tafida. Verbal abuse is just as damaging as physical abuse. Isn't it?"

Mrs. Tafida sighed. "What do you want?"

"I need to talk to her parents."

"We can't say anything like that to them," replied Mrs. Tafida, her tone sharpening.

"How come? Isn't our role to make sure the children have a healthy environment? They need to know their approach is harming the girl—and that it's going to erase her talent, her capacity, her dreams."

"Ms. Nour," said the principal, lowering her voice, "I know how much you care about Malika and the rest of the students. I admit you're one of the brightest teachers I've ever had, and I'm proud of you. But I am afraid this argument will cost you your job."

"Excuse me?"

"This is a private school with high tuition fees. Between you and me, what the administration cares about most are the parents' money and the school's reputation. If you anger the parents in any way—even if you're absolutely right—they'll pull their children and move them to other schools with no 'troublesome' teachers. The school will not tolerate that. So what happens is, they'll push you out to calm the parents down and protect the money."

"Oh God. This isn't an educational institution. It's a business."

"This is the bitter truth, dear. And it's not just here. It's every private school in this country. The public schools don't know the parents and don't care. They just care about avoiding trouble with the Ministry. So you need to live with it, if you want to keep your job."

"What about Malika?"

"Don't worry about her. She'll grow up like all the other children. What matters is her health and the certificate she'll get at the end. And even the certificate won't matter once she gets married. Talking to her parents won't change anything one iota. Put yourself first," said Mrs. Tafida.

Then she stood, signaling the meeting was over. "I have another meeting with the school owners. They want to know how many invitations I've sent to nurseries, sports clubs, toy stores, and hypermarkets for the upcoming orientation tour for new parents."

Nour stood up and shook her hand, lips pressed shut. She couldn't even thank her. She felt like she was walking out carrying a weight on her back. She had no idea how she was going to look Malika in the eye and what she was going to say after she had basically promised her during break that everything would be okay.

***

The bell rang, and kids' screams echoed through the building. It was dismissal time. Some waited for their parents to pick them up; others lined up for the school buses.

Nour watched Malika and Seif standing by the school's main gate, waiting for their mother. She decided, despite what she'd been warned, to try. She would talk to the mother anyway. Maybe, maybe, maybe.

"Excuse me, Madam," she said to Hala, who had just arrived.

"Hi. You're…?" Hala asked, trying to remember.

"I'm Ms. Nour, Malika's English teacher. Do you mind if I talk to you for a few minutes?"

"Uhm. Sure," Hala said reluctantly. She told the kids to get in the car.

Hala and Nour stood next to the car so they could keep an eye on them while talking.

"I won't take much of your time," said Nour.

"What did she do? I know she's a troublemaker," Hala said immediately.

"Not at all. She's a wonderful student. She's super intelligent and a fast learner."

"Is she?" Hala said, honestly surprised.

"Yes, she is. I just want to ask you a favor. I can tell from Malika's recent change in mood that she's depressed. It also shows in her questions and her reactions. She seems heavyhearted and devastated."

"Does she?" Hala scoffed. "This disturbing monkey is absolutely fine. She must've fooled you. I know my daughter better than anybody. If she's stopped asking questions like before, then I'm honestly relieved. She drives me crazy when she does."

"She hasn't fooled me," said Nour, softly. "We talked today during break. She feels hurt and alone because you insist on making her feel guilty for disappointing you. She has learned that asking questions is an act of disobedience."

"It is," Hala said, defensive. "And I'm glad she feels guilty. This stubborn girl needs to know there are rules, norms, and traditions that are not questionable."

"I'm sorry, madam," Nour said quietly, "but I'm afraid that's not true. What you've just said will make her grow into a helpless, submissive woman who can't stand up for herself."

Hala shot her a sharp look. "Now I understand where my child gets her rebellious ideas. You're uprooting what I'm trying to plant in her. You must be doing this to all the kids, too," she shouted, her voice rising loud enough to pull other parents' eyes toward them.

"Please lower your voice," Nour whispered. "The kids will hear what you're saying, and it's not true."

"How dare you talk to me like that? Don't you dare tell me what to do. Who do you think you are? You're just an employee we pay to teach our kids English. And I promise you this is your last day here," Hala yelled, getting into the driver's seat.

Hala's outburst created a little scene immediately. Heads turned. Parents whispered and retold what they'd just witnessed to the ones who had just arrived. A couple of students pointed and laughed. Two others lifted their phones to record the argument and take pictures of the red-faced teacher. Nour could see the principal standing at a distance, slowly shaking her head, side to side, like a slow-motion warning.

The sound of the car engine starting jolted Nour. She immediately turned to Malika. The girl was on her knees in the back seat, both hands pressed against the glass. Tears were streaming down her face. She knew—instantly—this was goodbye.

Right before the car moved, Malika watched Ms. Nour's lips form three silent words.

Be strong, dear.

Malika gave her a tearful smile. That small, shaky smile was the only thing that gave Nour hope as the car pulled away and disappeared past the crossroad—even though she knew she wasn't going to see Malika again.

From E to T

I've always loved train stations. I can't help imagining the stories of travelers from all walks of life. I like to guess what they do, where they're from, and why they're traveling. I never get tired of the atmosphere—even with the ear-piercing noise of dozens of footsteps pounding down the platforms as people run full speed to catch their trains, the high-pitched shouting of people trying to talk to each other while dragging their rolling bags, the kids' loud laughter and wild screaming as they zigzag around like frantic chickens, and the people yelling into their phones like the person on the other end is in another country.

I boarded the Alexandria–Cairo train and found my window seat. A woman with a baby on her lap sat in the aisle seat. I smiled at both of them as I slid past and sat down.

Even through the slightly dirty glass, I like sitting by the window. The train passes green fields and deserts, fancy villas and bare brick buildings, long lines of trees and piles of garbage, wealth and poverty. It's a story of Egypt from "E" to "T."

Across the aisle from me, in the same row, two young women were talking in very low voices. I remember them clearly. One had a reddish-brown pixie cut and a nose piercing. The other had a nape undercut dyed in shades of blue. Both looks were bold—bold enough to stand out in a car full of long hair, straightened hair, and bright headscarves. What I loved most was that neither of them seemed bothered by the people stealing glances at them, like they were some kind of public spectacle.

I felt the woman next to me turn her head and stare at them, then shake her head in that exaggerated, performative way that means: "Someone please notice how offended I am." She looked irritated, almost physically uncomfortable, like someone who suddenly has to pee and can't find a bathroom.

I was exhausted after a long day of running around Alexandria doing paperwork for my new job—signatures, stamps, more stamps to approve the stamps—and I let my head fall back against the seat. I was just about to fall asleep when I got interrupted.

"I ask Allah for His forgiveness. May He protect us and our children," the woman next to me murmured.

I opened my eyes and looked at her but said nothing. I wasn't sure if I was supposed to respond. Was she just praying out loud? Was she talking to me? Was this an invitation?

Her face made it clear she expected me to say something.

"Excuse me?" I finally asked.

"You see those devilish girls on my left?"

I glanced at the two girls, then looked back at her. "Yes. What about them?"

"Don't you see how weird they look?" She sounded shocked that I even had to ask.

Honestly, I didn't think they looked weird at all. They were minding their own business. Which is already more than I could say for us.

The woman kept staring at me, waiting.

"You mean—because of their haircuts?" I asked.

She turned her whole upper body toward me and leaned in. Her eyebrows were almost touching her hairline. She dropped her voice to a whisper like she was about to expose a national scandal.

"Don't you watch TV? There were posts on Facebook a few months ago with pictures of boys and girls like these holding rainbow flags at a music concert," she hissed. "Can you imagine? They want to ruin our society and mess with our customs and traditions. Thank God the police captured most of those bastards."

I knew exactly which incident she was talking about. To me, it was horrifying: they rounded up people at a concert—and even random people who were just nearby—simply because someone waved a rainbow flag. The whole thing felt absurd and cruel. The way the police behaved, and the way the talk shows reacted, you'd think aliens had invaded Cairo.

I didn't answer, so she kept going.

"You don't understand, dear, because you're obviously well-bred," she said. "Let me explain it to you. They're definitely *methleyeen* (queer). May God burn them all in hell. They're nonbelievers, *astaghfiru Allah*. I even have Christian friends who denounce them too. They want to poison our conservative Egyptian society. Of course they're funded by the West. The West wants us to rot and die."

I was stunned by how fast she'd jumped from haircuts to Western-funded moral collapse. This time, I couldn't just nod and let it pass.

"How can you tell someone's politics from their haircut?" I asked. "What harm have they done? They're just being themselves."

She reacted like I had insulted her personally. "You think we should wait until the harm is already done?" she snapped. "Of course not. I don't want my child to get infected or murdered."

Infected. Murdered.

My mind spun. The way she said it, you'd think there was a pack of zombies on board and we were all about to get eaten alive. She was clearly soaked in the same stuff that circulates here: social media pages, trash TV "talk shows," religious drama segments, tabloid-style panic. All of it pushing the same message—that queer people are not human.

Here, being LGBTQ means living underground. You blend in, you laugh at the same homophobic jokes as everyone else, you nod along when people call queer people "sick" and "perverted," and you keep your mouth shut so you can survive. You're expected to marry straight, especially if you're a man, so your family can sleep at night and your neighbors can't whisper. You do it to avoid being outed, humiliated, beaten, disappeared.

I thought of my friend Sameh and the way his face used to change whenever the guys in class made jokes about "those people," calling them "incomplete." Two of his classmates once followed him to the bathroom. They climbed onto the toilets in the stalls next to him and held their phones over the divider to take photos of him while he peed. They burst out laughing when he looked up and screamed.

After that, whenever people asked Sameh, "Why don't you have a girlfriend?" he started lying. He'd say, "I used to be in a relationship, but the other person let go." The boys always laughed at the "let go" part, because to them it meant Sameh must've been the weak one in the relationship. What they didn't know was that "the other person" was a boy named Khalid.

Sameh and Khalid had been in love since middle school. At first they didn't even have the words for it. They just knew something in them woke up around each other. They tried to shut it down. They tried to "behave." They suffered. They failed. Eventually, they stopped lying to themselves. They decided to secretly let themselves be in love—quietly, carefully, like a controlled flame.

They made plans. They were going to finish their last year of high school, apply for scholarships abroad, leave. Khalid had read about places where LGBTQ people live openly, where nobody tries to "correct" them.

Everything was going according to plan—until Khalid's mother overheard one of their phone calls.

She dragged Khalid to a therapist.

Like most so-called therapists here, the man told her that her son was biologically deformed, and that he could be "cured" if they "fixed his hormones." Medicate the gay away.

Sameh was luckier. His therapist accepted him. Sameh once told me that his doctor had only started to really understand after doing his PhD in the UK. At first, the doctor said, it was a cultural shock. But then he realized that people are not copies. They're not molded. It's not a "phase." It's not a "fix." The only "choice," he said, is this: you can come out in an Arab society and face harassment, humiliation, beatings, arrest — or you can keep it to yourself and rot quietly. That's not a cure. That's suffocation.

Khalid's mother didn't see it that way. She checked him into what she called "rehab," like he was an addict. She started the paperwork to send him to his father in Kuwait, convinced that the "problem" was the father's absence—that Khalid just needed "a man in the house." She didn't tell the father the truth about why she was sending him. She was afraid he would kill his own son to "wipe the shame."

By then, Khalid was on medications so heavy that he was shaking most of the time. He was barely present.

Shortly after they arrived in Kuwait, he took his own life.

Death is a fact none of us can bargain with. You can't argue your way out of it. Whether or not the person was close to you, death leaves a mark. Some people deny it and live like nothing happened until they crash into their own. Some people grieve so hard they stop living long before they actually die. Some people burn with anger and spend the rest of their lives trying to punish the world for it. And some people grieve quietly, take that death as their warning bell, turn their boat against the current, and try to carve out some kind of peace in the middle of chaos.

You can't rewrite the past. You can't stop what might happen in the future. All you really own—if you own anything—is the present moment you're in.

Sameh hasn't really healed. How could he? After Khalid died, he couldn't stand living in the shadows anymore. He applied for a scholarship after graduation, got accepted, and left for the United States to study for his BA and come out. I haven't seen him since, but we still talk. I wondered, sitting on that train, if the woman next to me had any idea what damage her words could do to someone like Khalid, someone who couldn't take it anymore.

"They're not a disease, ma'am," I finally said. "They're human beings. They have every right to exist. Live with it."

She looked at me like I had slapped her. Her face twisted—offended, disgusted, almost scared. It was like I had betrayed her just by refusing to agree.

Then, without a word to me, she stood up with the baby on her hip, grabbed her handbag, and snapped her fingers for the attendant.

"Find me another seat," she said loudly. "This place is filthy."

The attendant told her there was a free seat in Coach 7. That meant leaving business class to go sit in economy. She didn't care. She marched down the aisle and disappeared through the door.

When the door slammed shut, I felt my shoulders drop.

That's when I finally made eye contact with the two girls across the aisle. I didn't know if they'd heard the conversation or not. But we smiled at one another. I couldn't even explain the relief I felt— like someone had quietly put a hand on my back and said, "I see you."

After I exhaled, I turned back to the window.

The train kept cutting through fields and ruins, glass towers and crumbling rooftops. Egypt from "E" to "T," passing by in seconds.

Because They Can

"Please go to page seven. Can someone describe what's in the picture at the bottom?" Rahma asked slowly, making sure everyone could follow.

Her students were adult English learners, ages twenty-one to thirty-five. They were in this class for different reasons: to improve their English, to get a certificate, to qualify for jobs that demanded "some English," even if they'd never actually have to use it. Mostly, they wanted one more line on a resumé—one more argument to escape to a city with better jobs.

Rahma lived in a district that felt like a small village. A maze of alleys where everyone knew everyone. Family news traveled by mouth before it even happened. Privacy didn't exist. The buildings were so close you could literally lean over your balcony and shake hands with the neighbor across. Thin shared walls meant you didn't just hear arguments—you could hear stomach gas. So even if you tried not to share your business, your walls shared it for you.

Rahma went to a nearby public school where cheating was basically an unofficial policy, because if students failed in large numbers the Ministry of Education would send inspectors and make trouble. She was lucky, though, because every summer—ever since primary one—she stayed with her aunt Nawal in Giza.

Rahma adored Nawal. Nawal was the only person who had ever really seen her. Nawal and her husband, Ashraf, loved Rahma like their own child.

"God didn't give me children," Nawal would tell her, "but He gave me you—his *rahma* (mercy)."

When Rahma was born, her father, Abbas, was furious that the baby was a girl. He refused to name her at first, then offered names that showed how disgusted he was, like *Hozn* (sadness). Because of that, Nawal stepped in and named her. Nawal was also the reason Rahma was not circumcised. When Abbas tried to force it, Ashraf threatened to cut off the money he regularly sent Abbas. That was the only thing that stopped him. Abbas could say no to a daughter, but not to cash.

Every summer, Rahma went back from Giza with new dresses, T-shirts, blouses, and pants she would never have been allowed to wear in the alley. Abbas wasn't told, of course. "My father would kill me," she would whisper to Nawal.

Nawal hired private tutors to teach Rahma English when she was still young. Abbas was against spending a single pound on Rahma's education. In his mind, educating a girl was a waste. She'll just get married in the end. But he backed off every time Nawal reminded him what would happen to his monthly "support" if he refused.

To Abbas, money was more valuable than his daughter. Honestly, that was the only good thing he thought her birth had brought him. He was constantly burnt out and wired at the same time—drugs, alcohol, and three packs of cigarettes a day don't come cheap. His tiny 2,000 EGP salary couldn't cover all that.

So Nawal found workarounds. She slipped extra money to Rahma's mother, Magda, in secret—hidden in clothing, tucked inside food bags.

Magda, meanwhile, locked Rahma in her bedroom every night before Abbas came home drunk, high, or both. She used to tell Nawal, "I wish Rahma were a boy so she could protect herself. I'm terrified I won't be able to save her from that heartless man I'm married to."

Rahma kept spending more time with Nawal—not just summers anymore—once she got into Cairo University. By twenty-two, she wasn't just fluent; she loved the language. She started dreaming of teaching English in her own neighborhood, to the kids who couldn't even spell their names in English letters.

After graduation, she taught for three years in private language centers. Then Ashraf referred her to a friend at USAID, and she joined a program teaching English to young learners. She felt, for once, like her life was finally hers.

Then Abbas showed up.

He had heard at work—he kept the books at the Ministry of Irrigation—that a wealthy fifty-year-old Kuwaiti businessman in their governorate was "looking to marry." Abbas immediately told his coworker to put in a word: "I have a daughter. She's available. High dowry only. Cash. In dinar."

A few days later, Abbas got a call. The businessman was interested. A driver would pick him up in the morning.

The meeting went better than well. Abbas agreed to the marriage on the spot. He didn't bother to ask basic questions first— things any Egyptian family is supposed to ask. Is the man already married? Does he have other wives? Is he sick? Dying? Violent? Is he even who he says he is? Abbas didn't care if the man was a criminal or a saint. He cared about the money.

Nawal and Ashraf tried to stop it. They had been able to protect Rahma before by using financial leverage, but this time they weren't richer than the groom.

"It's nonnegotiable," Abbas told Rahma. "Your *dokhla* is next Friday."

Dokhla is the word families use for the consummation of the marriage. The wedding night. The word alone made Rahma feel like her body had been laid out on a table for inspection and purchase. Exposed. Naked.

Rahma begged him not to do this. It didn't matter. Abbas had already signed the marriage contract in the groom's home, in front of the *ma'zoun*—the notary who legally registers a marriage. Under Egyptian personal status law, her father could legally sign on her behalf. Her "consent" was just paperwork. The *ma'zoun* got paid extra to skip the part where he's supposed to ask the bride directly: "Do you accept this man as your husband?" A "no" should have stopped the marriage. But there's no such thing as "no" when money is involved and conscience is gone.

"Am I that cheap in your eyes?" Rahma cried. "You practically sold me. I have a say in this. I don't want to get married—not to that man and not like this!"

Abbas slapped her, hard, across the face.

"You will marry him," he shouted. "Your loose life at your aunt's is over. I actually pity the man, marrying someone as useless as you. Now pack your rags. His driver will pick you up tomorrow night. May you never come back."

For Abbas, it was perfect. He didn't have to lift a finger, didn't have to pay one pound for wedding furniture or gold like other fathers did. The groom even had Abbas's house renovated—fresh paint, new tiles—which Abbas bragged about to anyone who would listen. The groom's "connections" also got Abbas promoted at work. Abbas walked around like a man who had finally won.

Rahma, meanwhile, was living in a nightmare.

She couldn't stand the man who was, on paper, her husband. She recoiled from his touch. He beat her and forced himself on her anyway. She tried so hard to convince herself to surrender, to "be a good wife," to survive it. She couldn't.

She started lying about her period—saying it came twice, sometimes three times in one month—so he would leave her alone.

One night she showed up at her parents' door, banging nonstop until Magda opened.

Rahma's blouse was ripped. Her arms and face were bruised and bleeding.

Magda screamed. "What happened? What did he do to you?"

Rahma told her.

She'd come home early and heard laughter coming from her bedroom. She crept toward the door and opened it to find her husband in their bed with two other women. She froze. He turned, saw her, and his face changed—not guilty, not ashamed. Dangerous.

He jumped out of bed like a lion in a hunt. He grabbed her, slapped her again and again, dragged her by the arm. He hurled insults she'd never even heard before. He punched and kicked her in front of the two women, who stayed on the bed and watched in silence.

Then he dragged her by both arms across the floor, all the way to the front door, and kicked her out into the hallway like garbage.

Magda cleaned her up and helped her change her clothes. When Abbas came home after midnight and saw Rahma there, he didn't even ask if she was okay. He exploded.

"Are you out of your mind?" he yelled. "What did you do to make the man that angry? You must have said something stupid, like always. Did you even take his permission to come here? What am I supposed to tell him now? You filthy whore…"

He kept cursing at her—and at Magda, for letting her in—for "disrespecting" her husband by leaving his house.

A week later, the doorbell rang and rang and rang. Abbas stormed over to yell at whoever was leaning on the bell. He opened the door to find a police officer and two security men.

"Is Rahma Abbas here?" the officer asked.

Abbas shook with fear. He didn't answer.

The officer pushed past him and stepped inside. "Go get her," he told the guards.

"What did she do, pasha?" Abbas stammered.

"We have an order of arrest. We're to take her back to her husband's home now."

In Egypt, a husband can file what's called a *beit al-ta'a* case—"house of obedience." It basically says: my wife left, bring her back. The police will literally come to your parents' door, take you like a runaway criminal, and deliver you back to the man. Courts here drag on for years, sometimes decades—unless the man is rich or connected. Then it moves very fast.

It's the same system that excuses a man who kills his wife "for honor," but would execute a wife for killing her husband for the same reason. Men who cheat get "a second chance." Women who cheat get a funeral.

They took Rahma out of the apartment like she was under arrest, pushed her into a police car, and disappeared with her. Her mother didn't hear from her for weeks.

And then, suddenly, Rahma came back.

When Magda opened the door, her daughter was standing there with the same little suitcase she'd left with—and wearing a bright red dress.

"Thank God you're alive," Magda cried. "I thought he had done something to you."

"God finally answered my prayers," Rahma said, with the smallest smile. "He's dead."

"You killed him?"

"I wish I had. He died in a plane crash coming from Bahrain."

Rahma had to stay home for three months after that. The local sheikh told Magda it was required: the '*idda*, the mourning period a widow must complete—even if she doesn't consider him anything but her abuser. Rahma refused to wear black at first. "There's nothing to mourn," she said. But Magda begged her. "Please. Do it for me. They'll eat us alive with gossip."

During that time, Abbas was in prison. The police had raided his office and found 50,000 EGP in the drawer. Someone had snitched—probably a coworker who was angry Abbas wouldn't split it with him. Abbas got three years for ill-gotten money.

Rahma waited out the three months like a prisoner doing her last stretch. Then she reapplied for her old job. Her boss welcomed her back and assigned her to teach in a newly opened language center in her district.

Magda still worried about talk. "People are saying your daughter stopped wearing black," two neighbors whispered to her. "People are saying she thinks she's free now." Nawal tried, as always, to defend Rahma. She told Magda, "She needs air. After what she went through, the least you can do is stop making it worse."

Rahma felt alive in front of a whiteboard. That's where she felt like herself. She was nervous her first day back, but it faded fast. The students—mostly adults—respected her. Two years went by like that, and for the first time since everything, she could breathe again. People in class even told her they admired her English. That mattered more than she let them see. It meant she could be more than what the alley said she was.

"Now go to page seven," she said in class one evening. "Who would like to describe what's in the picture at the bottom?"

A young man shot his hand in the air. "I see *gerliz and boys and a bitch," he said proudly.

Rahma blushed. "Thank you, Ahmed. Yes—there are girls and boys on the beach." She carefully repeated each word with the right sounds, especially the last one. Then she added, "It's important to pronounce consonants and vowels correctly, or else the word might change completely. For example—"

She turned to the whiteboard and wrote as she spoke.

"'Cat,' 'car,' and 'case' don't share the same vowel. Their sounds are /æ/, /ɑː/, and /eɪ/."

"*Sank you, *tetchar," one of them told her. "We *teached *Englesh *vawels is *fife!"

Her eyes were apologetic, embarrassed.

Rahma smiled. "It's not your fault, Amal. Unfortunately, in this country, English is taught like math—something to memorize for the exam—instead of as a language. Schools care that you memorize lists of words and grammar rules so you can pass the final test. That's why our team here is trying to change the system, even if it's just a little. Doing something is better than doing nothing."

They nodded, thanked her in Arabic, and left.

Now only two people were in the room: Rahma, and the one she'd been avoiding looking at—Ramzy.

He walked toward her desk. Rahma kept her head down like she was still busy organizing papers.

"Nobody's here," he said softly. "Don't worry."

"This is my workplace, Ramzy," she whispered. "We cannot talk here."

"I know. I'll wait for you outside. Take your time."

He left.

Rahma watched him go, breathing in the trace of his cologne hanging in the air. She stared at the empty doorway. Her eyes filled.

She was the one who had texted him that they needed to talk. And now that he was here, her mind was blank.

She finally left the building and found him in his car. She looked both ways, looked up at the center's windows to make sure no one was watching, and then she got in.

"Please drive away from here," she said.

"Sure," he said gently. "Just take it easy."

"I wish it were that easy." She looked at him for a second, then out the window again. "My family still says it's not possible."

Ramzy parked at the corner, turned to her, and frowned. "What's not possible?"

"Our marriage, Ramzy," she said, barely above a whisper.

"Why? I have a job. I have an apartment. I can afford to support us. And I love you, Rahma. You know I do." He took her hand.

"I told them all of that," she said. "Except the love part. They don't care about that. Their problem is the seven-year gap."

"What difference does it make if one of us is older?"

"You know what difference it makes here. I wish you were older than me. Not the other way around. My family is terrified of talk. They still give me a hard time for working. To them, a widow should spend the rest of her life grieving for her husband… even if that 'husband' was basically a buyer. And now I'll get dragged for wanting to marry a man who's younger than me. Even my brother will say no."

"Your brother doesn't get a say in this."

"He does."

"How?"

"My parents gave him a carte blanche the minute he started school and learned how to talk like a thug. He copies the boys around him, and they treat him like the little man of the house. His gender gives him power. This place gives him power."

Ramzy went quiet. She could see in his face that he had a lot to say, and he was swallowing it for her sake.

"There's a café around the corner," he offered. "Let's grab something to eat and talk."

"What if somebody sees us?"

"Come on, Rahma. We're adults. We're not doing anything wrong."

"I am scared to death, Ramzy. I've had enough of the staring and the insults."

"Why don't you just ignore them?" he asked. "You have the right to be happy. You have the right to choose your life. It's your call, not theirs."

"We're not living in a fancy compound in New Cairo where everybody pretends to be open-minded and modern," she said. "We're in an alley that keeps records. People here know who I was at six years old, at thirteen, at twenty-two. They've memorized me."

"You can come back with me to Cairo," he said quietly. "I talked to my family about you. They can't wait to meet you. They can't believe someone like you has managed to survive here."

"Do they know about the age gap?"

"Yes. Our story reminded them of when they were young. My mom is two months older than my dad. Their families made a scene about it. But they got married anyway."

Rahma let out a breath. "I wish I'd grown up in a family like yours."

"Then let's leave this place," he said. "We shouldn't stay where we don't belong."

"You mean elope?" she asked, eyebrows raised.

"I mean we get married in the nearest city and then go to Cairo together."

She stared at him.

"Rahma," he said softly, "you trust me, don't you? You know I would never hurt you. I would never force you to do anything."

"I know, Ramzy. I just feel lost. And helpless."

"You're not helpless," he said. "You're strong enough to stand up for what you deserve. You can do this. You deserve this."

"It's not that easy," she said. "Not in a place that raises girls to be owned. Here, women get handed over—from fathers, brothers, and uncles to husbands. When the husband dies, the woman is 'returned' to her original owners, like an item. I was literally sold by my father. My own father. And women here still get denied inheritance, even though it's illegal and even though religion says they have a share. People just say, 'Why should a woman inherit? She'll leave and join another family.' Ignorance has eaten these people until there's nothing left."

"I know," he said quietly. "That's why my family left before I was even born. And when I graduated and started doing business here, they were terrified. They've seen what this place does to people like you."

He took a breath.

"I want us to leave," he said. "Just you and me. You need to live somewhere that lets you breathe."

"You talk about Cairo like it's heaven," she said, almost smiling.

"No place is heaven," he said. "But we can make our own. I have friends in New Cairo, Sheikh Zayed, New Giza. They say you can have privacy there. Space. No one watching you from the balcony, no one reporting you to your own mother."

"What about my family?" she asked.

"I'm afraid," he said, "there's nothing left to *say* to them. You've already said everything. Now it's about what you're willing to do. Look at your parents. They made their choices. They're living the lives they chose—or, honestly, the lives their choices forced on them. There's always this silent agreement in families like this: parents get to control your life because you're 'their blood.' It's like a lifetime ownership contract, especially for daughters. Your mother gave in to her own nightmare. Don't let them make you live theirs."

He swallowed.

"And if your choice leaves me out," he added, "I'll live with that. I just don't want you to abandon yourself for them."

Rahma looked at him, and for a moment she saw him the way she always did: the only man in her life who had ever stood *with* her, not *over* her.

His words echoed in her head as she turned toward the car window and stared down the narrow street. She thought of Robert Frost:

Two roads diverged in a wood, and I –

I took the one less traveled by,

And that has made all the difference.

She'd always wondered if there was any road other than the one she'd been pushed down.

Now, for the first time, she could see it.

Maybe not just one road.

Maybe more than one.

If she dared.

One Day

The brief silent gaps between the ventilator beeps in the ICU are more terrifying than the beeps themselves. Every pause makes my heart drop into my stomach.

I held her cold hand and sobbed. Her hands have always been so warm, even on the coldest nights. Now she'd been in the hospital for a week, and the doctors still didn't know if she'd wake up. She'd barely survived the car crash after leaving the house. I knew she'd been crying when she left. Crying because of me. The guilt is killing me. I keep wondering if I did this to her.

The hardest fights are the ones you have with yourself. The way your own mind turns on you afterward. My mind keeps replaying everything I said, mocking how childish I sounded, how stubborn I was, how petty. The voice in my head won't stop. It keeps punishing me until I feel sick with shame. If you're that wise, dear mind, why didn't you stop me before I said it? Why do you show up only after I've already broken something?

Yes, I'm guilty. Fine. But I am willing to change. Just let me. I just need her back.

When we first met at work, Hanan was bright. Lively. Positive. Independent—but not in a way that made men "uncomfortable," as they say. People went to her with their problems. She listened, really listened, in a way that made you feel lighter after talking to her. She was exactly the kind of woman I get attached to, and also the kind of woman I tell myself I shouldn't marry because "strong women become bossy." That's what I used to say.

But unlike anyone before her, Hanan put me first. She gave things up for me. She did it out of love.

Everybody liked her. Everybody respected her. That bothered me.

I couldn't stand seeing her talk to other men in the company. So when we started dating, the first thing I asked her to do was to stop chatting with them. She argued, of course. She said it made work awkward. She said it wasn't fair. In the end, she stopped anyway—because she didn't want to hurt my feelings.

People at work noticed immediately. She kept more distance. She laughed less. She no longer stayed in the hallway talking to the guys. I felt proud. Proud, like I had won. Like every other man would now understand that she was mine. I didn't even question what it was doing to her.

The one thing I never understood about her was her mood before her period. She called it her "PMS week." It actually took months for her to even say the word to me, because she said it was embarrassing. Here, a woman can't even buy pads at a pharmacy without wanting the female pharmacist, and even then the pads get double-bagged—first in a black plastic bag, then hidden in the pharmacy's white bag like contraband. You don't talk about your body. You're trained to hide it.

My friends told me, "Avoid her those days. Don't talk to her when she's like that. Women get crazy before their period. It's a nightmare." One of my closest friends said, "Better yet, don't get married at all. Marriage is a trap. Women change the second you tie the knot. They stop looking the same. They're moody. They fight for no reason. Stay free, brother."

I heard him. I didn't listen. Not then.

Before our wedding, Hanan submitted her resignation and gave three months' notice. Our company has a policy: no employees can marry each other. Of course she was the one who had to leave. I'm the man. I "can't" lose my job. Her family would've called off the wedding if I did. She quit even though she was about to get promoted. It wasn't even a discussion. It was "normal." I'm supposed to be the breadwinner. A man with no job is shame. A woman with no job is "devoted."

We said—we agreed—she'd look for a new job after the wedding.

But she didn't have the time. She was busy furnishing our apartment. I "couldn't" go with her because I "hate shopping." So I told her I was busy, even when I wasn't. My mother went with her instead—to "help," and to "make sure the budget stays reasonable," and to "make sure the taste is right," which means my mother decided what the couch should look like, what bed we should sleep in, and what plates we would eat from. I listened to all the complaints from both sides, but I didn't step in. I didn't want to pick a side. I just wanted peace.

Hanan got pregnant one month after the wedding. We had agreed to wait. When she mentioned abortion, I lost it. I told her, "We can't reject God's will."

After that, she became more emotional, more easily hurt, more demanding. At least, that's how I described it in my head. She said she was exhausted and lonely. She said she felt trapped at home. I didn't hear it then.

Hanan was never someone who could sit in a house all day for weeks. She'd always worked. Suddenly she was stuck cooking, cleaning, doing laundry, alone, pregnant, while I went to work and "provided." I told myself I was doing my job. I told myself she should be grateful.

Then our son, Waseem, was born. She loved him, completely. And somehow it broke her at the same time. She started losing pieces of the woman I first met. I didn't see it. Or I didn't want to.

"Here's pappy," my sister Sarah whispered as she opened the door. She walked in with Waseem. I hadn't even heard them knock. My mother followed them into the ICU room. She looked at me with that pity she does—the kind that's not really pity; it's judgment pretending to care. Then she rolled her eyes.

I felt her looking at my hand holding Hanan's hand. I let go immediately, because I didn't have the energy for one of my mother's comments about how "soft" I am.

Waseem ran to me and climbed into my lap.

"*Teita* says Mommy is leaving us," he said, his voice shaking. "Is that true, pappy?"

"Of course not," I said. "She's just sick. She's not leaving us."

Waseem spun toward my mother. "See, *teita*? I told you so."

Then he looked back at me. "Auntie Sarah told me she's here because I don't drink milk. Is that true?"

I looked at Sarah. She nodded like, Yes, go with that.

"Definitely," I said.

Waseem has her eyes. Hanan's eyes. Warm, hazel, always looking right into you. When he looks at me like that, listening with his whole face, I can't breathe. Tears started slipping down my face.

My mother hissed. She grabbed Waseem by the arm. "Go outside with Sarah," she told him. "She'll get you juice and cookies from the cafeteria."

"I don't want to," he said. "I just want Mommy."

"I said GO," she snapped. "Be a good boy."

His head dropped. He let Sarah lead him out of the room.

The second the door closed, I knew it was coming.

"What's wrong with you?" my mother said. "Men don't cry. Don't be weak in front of your son. You want him to grow up weak like you?"

"I'm not weak, Mama," I said. "My wife is dying in front of me. She's here because of me."

"No she's not. She's here because she's stupid and stubborn."

"She's not stupid," I shot back. "Why do you hate her so much? She's treated you like a mother since the day we married. Her own mother died before the wedding. She gave you that place."

"Exactly," my mother said. "She's bad luck. Death follows her. Your father died after you married her, too."

"Seriously?" I said. "You actually believe that?"

"Yes. And now she's being punished. God is teaching her a lesson for leaving her husband's house."

"If God is teaching anyone a lesson, it's me," I said. "I'm the one who pushed her past the limit."

"Why?" she demanded. "For what? You have the right to marry three more women if you want. She has no right to object. She should have been grateful to have a man like you."

"I don't want anyone else," I said quietly. "That was a mistake. A stupid mistake. I know that now. Hanan is proud. She couldn't stand the idea of being cheated on, even emotionally. I just want her to wake up. I just want another chance."

Before my mother could answer, Hanan coughed.

I froze. She blinked—once, twice.

I rushed to her bed. "Hanan. *Habibti*. Can you hear me? Please. Say anything. Move your hand. Just show me you're here. Please wake up. Everything will be okay, I swear. Just forgive me."

A tear slid down her cheek. Her eyelids fluttered. Her mouth pulled up, just a little. Almost a smile.

"*Alhamdulillah*," I whispered. "You're okay. We're okay, *habibti*. We're okay."

***

Two years later

"How many times do I have to say it?" I shouted. "No nannies

88

in this house. I don't want strangers raising my kids."

Hanan whispered, "First, please lower your voice. The kids are sleeping. Second, I'm not asking for a live-in nanny. I'm asking for help with Hana for a few hours while I'm at work. Waseem will be back from school after I'm home. You know how hard it was to find someone willing to hire me with that huge unemployment gap on my resumé."

"First," I snapped, mocking her tone, "I'll talk however I want in my own house. Second, I don't care about your job. You're not going to work. Your family is your only priority. These high dreams you have are going to break your neck. You need to learn to compromise."

Her eyes filled. "Learn to compromise?" she whispered. "Really? You're saying that to me?"

"You're selfish," I said. "You want everything. You should be thankful you have me and your kids. Other women wish they had half of what you have."

"Why do you sound like your mother?" she asked.

"Leave my mother out of this," I shot back. "And for the record, she was always right about you being stubborn and selfish. You know what? I should've married the other woman. She would've been more obedient. And more interesting than you."

"So I'm the problem?" Hanan asked.

"Yes," I said. "Ever since we got married, you've turned boring, toxic, and ugly. You don't care about my needs. You only care about the kids."

"Are you serious?" she said. "Aren't the kids yours too? And what about my needs? Have you ever thought about those? Have you ever thought you might be the reason I'm not the same woman you first met?"

"It's your fault," I said. "All of this is your fault."

She stared at me.

"You caged me," she said. "You built walls around me. You cut me off from my work, my friends, my life. I disappeared for you. I erased myself for you. And now you're telling me *you're* the victim? At least I've been faithful."

"I'd kill you if you weren't," I said.

"Oh, I know," she said. "Your pride. Your honor. Your image. If I ever looked at someone else, you'd call it shame. But you? You almost married someone else while I was still in the house, and somehow I'm supposed to swallow it? My honor doesn't count?"

"You bitch," I snapped. "I have the right to marry three more women if I want."

"Trust me," she said, looking straight at me, "no woman will ever be enough for you. You'll take another happy, alive woman and turn her into what you just called me."

"I have the right to see other women," I said. "You pushed me there. You made me feel like I needed someone else to make me feel alive again. That's on you."

"Go ahead," she said. "Marry four who will 'make you happy.' I'm telling you now: I won't be one of them."

She held my eyes for a long second. Then she turned and walked to our bedroom.

The door closed.

I stood there in the living room, breathing hard, full of heat. But under it, there it was again—that voice. The one I hate. The one that tells the truth.

I know I went too far.

I know I've been going too far.

I know I helped make her into what she is now. I know I chipped away at her and called the pieces "peace." I know I trained myself to enjoy saying no. There's a sick kind of pleasure in control. In being the one who decides. In making her a "ring on my finger," like people say here—something owned.

If I were her, I would have asked me for a divorce a long time ago.

But I also know what I would have done if she had asked.

I would've said no.

I would've refused just because I could.

I don't know why I'm like this. I don't know why I keep doing the same old things even when something deep inside me is telling me I'll regret it.

One day, I'll regret it.

One day.

But not today.

At 7:00 PM

It was an ordinary night at the grocery store where Layla worked the evening shift to pay her bills. In the mornings, ever since COVID, she taught online—but that income didn't even cover rent for her studio. The grocery job barely plugged the hole.

Some nights were fine. Some nights were the kind that made her question why she was even still here. Customers barked at her. Treated her like she wasn't human. And this was one of those days. She felt wrung out.

Then she felt someone watching her.

A young woman was standing in line. Mask on. Curly hair. Eyes like warmth. Color everywhere—in the hair, in the clothes, in the way she stood. Something about her felt alive. Layla felt, for a second, like she'd been standing naked in the dark and someone had finally switched the light on.

"She knows I'm gay," Layla thought. "Is she, too?"

"Hi. How are you?" the woman asked. Her voice was soft and musical.

"I'm good, thank you. How are you?" Layla answered, but her

heart had started racing.

Layla wanted to keep talking but didn't know how to do it without sounding obvious.

"Do you, by any chance, have Middle Eastern roots?" Layla asked.

The woman smiled with her eyes. "Kind of," she said. "And you?"

"I do," Layla said. She was barely feeling the groceries in her hands anymore. She couldn't even remember what she was scanning. All she could see were those eyes. They looked kind—but also unreadable.

"My ex-girlfriend is Middle Eastern," the woman said from behind the plexiglass divider.

Layla felt butterflies explode in her stomach at the word ex-girlfriend. So she's queer. Oh my God. She's queer.

Layla wished, in that moment, that there were no other customers in the world. Just them, talking forever. But the receipt printed. Layla had to hand it to her.

"I know some Arabic words," the woman said playfully as she picked up her bag. "*Ana bahebbak* (I love you)," she said then walked away smiling.

After that, Layla couldn't stop smiling either. Even when she wasn't supposed to.

They talked a few more times over the next days—just a few exchanges at the register, nothing long. But for Layla, it was oxygen. She hadn't felt happy like that in a long time. She promised herself that next time, she'd ask her name.

Every day at 7:00 PM, Layla would start waiting.

The woman always seemed to come after seven. So Layla made sure to take her bathroom break at 6:45, fix her hair, calm down, breathe. Seven o'clock became sacred.

One night, around 7:30, a gay couple was checking out at a different register. Layla was focused on her scanner when she suddenly felt someone's breath too close to her ear.

"Look at those two," her manager whispered.

Layla's stomach dropped. She already knew where this was going. He leaned in even closer and muttered, "The one in the red shirt is the 'woman,' of course. *Allah yehra'on.* May God burn them."

Layla stared at the register screen and said nothing.

She had left a place that tried to erase her, only to end up working next to people who spoke the same way—just lower, just in whispers, just in code. Back home, people felt free to say it out loud and call it morals. Here they hid it because they were scared of the law.

So Layla kept quiet at work. She never mentioned that she was queer. She'd heard coworkers laugh at people who didn't fit their idea of "normal." Sometimes she wanted to snap, to tell them they were cruel, to defend whoever they were mocking. But she didn't. She didn't want to out herself by accident. She told herself: soon, I'll find something safer.

Until then, she survived on small kindness. The customers who treated her like a human being. The ones who asked how her day was. And, most of all, her.

At 7:55 PM that night—just when Layla was starting to lose hope—she saw her.

The girl winked. Layla almost forgot how to speak.

This time, Layla noticed what she was buying: cat food.

"Oh, you have a cat?" Layla asked, trying not to sound too eager. "I love cats."

The woman smiled. "I'm trying new food to see if she'll like it."

Layla surprised herself with how much she talked after that. She never opened up to customers. But with this woman, it just spilled out. She told her about her research, her studies, her travels. The woman actually listened—really listened—and asked Layla to write down the title of the article she'd recently published. Layla wrote it. And under it, she wrote her name and email.

She wanted to write her number, too. But she didn't want to come off the wrong way. She didn't want to scare her.

"What's your name?" Layla finally asked.

"Tina," she said, smiling like always. "I'll read your article. See you soon."

That night, Layla floated.

Seven o'clock wasn't just a time anymore. It was the hour her heart came back to life.

Then Tina disappeared.

A week went by. Then two. Then a month.

Layla still watched the door every night. She scanned faces for curly hair. For that pink hat Tina once wore. For those eyes. Every time someone even slightly looked like her, Layla's heart jumped. And then dropped. She checked her email constantly, even her spam folder, hoping to see Tina's name. Nothing.

She missed someone she barely knew. It felt ridiculous. It felt dramatic. It also felt real.

She replayed their moments together in her head. Tina's voice calling her "*habibti*" in Arabic, half-joking. The way she leaned in.

The way her energy made the whole store feel less gray. Layla kept listening to "Find You" by Nick Jonas on the train and imagining telling Tina about it. She kept thinking, Next time I'll ask for her number. Next time I'll ask for coffee. Next time.

But there hadn't been a next time.

She started to wonder: Did Tina feel anything, or was I alone in this? Was it all in my head? Am I just lonely and projecting?

She remembered a line from Paulo Coelho: "Waiting is painful. Forgetting is painful. But not knowing which to do is the worst kind of suffering."

A month later, Layla went to the bathroom, washed her face, and came back to find Tina—right there—checking out at another register.

Layla's stomach twisted. She didn't even know what she was feeling. Relief. Panic. Joy. Hurt.

Tina wasn't looking at her.

Layla waited. Tina kept her eyes down, like she was somewhere else completely. Her smile, when it finally appeared, was softer now. Sad. Her whole face had changed. She looked like somebody carrying something heavy.

When she finished paying, Tina walked past Layla's lane.

"Hi," she said.

"It's been a long time since I last saw you," Layla managed. What she wanted to say was: I missed you.

"Yeah," Tina said. "I usually come when it's quiet and less busy."

That stung. Layla heard it in her bones. So you've been coming at different times. Are you… avoiding me?

"I read your article, by the way," Tina said. "It's really good."

Layla barely registered the compliment. Something was off. This wasn't the same Tina who had lit up the room. This Tina felt… far away. Guarded. Hurt.

Layla wanted to ask, Are you okay? Who did this to you? Can I fix it? But she didn't want to cross a line that wasn't hers.

Instead she swallowed, took a breath, and did the bravest thing she'd done in months.

"I was wondering," she said, voice shaking a little, "if you'd want to get coffee sometime."

Tina's face shifted. Surprise, yes. But not shock. Like she'd been expecting this. Like she'd both hoped for it and dreaded it.

"Yes," Tina said softly. "We can get coffee."

Layla felt her heart jump.

"Can I save your number?" she asked.

"Yes," Tina said.

Layla gave her phone. Tina typed.

Then Layla asked, half-teasing, half-terrified, "Do you remember my name?"

"Um…" Tina hesitated.

That one tiny pause hurt more than Layla expected. Tina didn't remember her name.

They said goodbye. Layla should have felt ecstatic—she finally had Tina's number—but something in her stomach felt twisted. Wrong. Off.

Later that night, Layla texted. Thank you for giving me your number. When are you free for that coffee?

No answer.

Minutes passed. Then hours.

Layla stared at her screen, feeling stupid. Of course she texted too soon. Of course she pushed.

Finally, a reply came.

Tina's message was warm, but formal. Careful. She said her life was complicated right now. She said she wasn't looking for anything. She said she wasn't in a place to get involved.

Layla read the message again and again. She understood. She

really did. She could feel the pain behind the words. She wanted to text back: I don't need anything from you. I just want you not to feel alone. I can wait. I can hold space. I can just sit with you in the quiet. I can be safe.

But Tina was already pulling back.

Layla had to respect that. Even if it felt like losing something she hadn't really gotten to have.

After that, Layla walked through her days like a half-version of herself. She replayed the last month in her head, trying to figure out if she'd imagined it all. Was Tina really the sun after the storm, or did Layla just need someone to feel like sun? Was it in her head? Was it real? Does it matter if it was real only to her?

She thought about quitting the job just so Tina wouldn't feel watched. She didn't. Instead, she wrote.

She sat alone in her tiny apartment and wrote about Tina—the way she walked, the way her presence softened the edges of a horrible day, the way, for a few minutes at a checkout counter, Layla felt seen.

She didn't know if writing it down was her way of letting go or her way of keeping Tina forever.

All she knew was that what she felt was beautiful. Honest. She hadn't felt something like that in years.

She wished they had met somewhere else. Sometime else. Somewhere safe, where neither of them had to be careful.

Why were they meant to meet at all?

7:00 PM became the hour when Layla's heart dies every night—and then comes back to life again, with the memory of Tina.

About the Author

Mahitab Mahmoud is an author and educator whose work centers on identity, silence, queerness, and the emotional cost of living between cultures. In both *When Silence Shatters* and *The Color of Our Names*, she explores the quiet tensions that shape lives lived under expectation, secrecy, and social constraint. Through layered storytelling, she examines what happens when silence becomes survival—and what it costs to finally break it.

Mahitab is the author of *When Silence Shatters: A Collection of Short Stories*, a finalist for the 2025 Wishing Shelf Book Awards and recipient of multiple 5-star reviews from Readers' Favorite. *The Color of Our Names* continues this exploration through interconnected lives navigating oppression, longing, and belonging across Egypt and its diaspora. Across her work, she asks what it means to be seen, to survive emotionally, and to claim space in societies that demand silence.